NEVER STARE AT A GRIZZLY BEAR

and other animal poems by

Nick Toczek

Illustrated by David Parkins

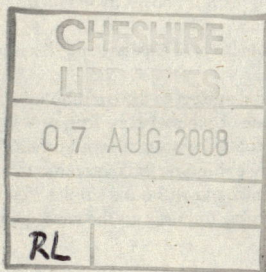

MACMILLAN CHILDREN'S BOOKS

For Gaynor and our children, Becci and Matt.

Also for Mrs Davison and the rest of the staff at Rawdon Littlemoor School in Leeds, and for the pupils (1995-8), for whom several of these poems were specifically written.

First published 2000
by Macmillan Children's Books
a division of Macmillan Publishers Limited
20 New Wharf Road, London N1 9RR
Basingstoke and Oxford
www.panmacmillan.com

Associated companies throughout the world

ISBN 0 330 39121 6

5 7 9 8 6 4

A CIP catalogue record for this book is available from the British Library.

Printed by Mackays of Chatham plc, Chatham, Kent.

Nick Toczek works as a poet, storyteller, journalist, lecturer and novelist. He performs the world's fastest poem and does magic tricks too. In the past 30 years he has made over 20,000 public appearances and most recently has been touring with his Million-Miles-An-Hour Show. He lives in Bradford with his wife and two children.

David Parkins has illustrated numerous books, ranging from maths textbooks to *The Beano*. His picture books have been shortlisted for the Smarties Book Prize and the Kurt Maschler Award. He lives in Lincoln with his wife, three children and six cats.

Contents

Never Stare at a Grizzly Bear

You can stand and stare at a teddy bear,
Glower and glare without a care;
But it's only fair to make you aware
That a grizzly bear is a different affair.

Yes, a grizzly bear is a different affair.
Friendly ones are fairly rare.
Believe me, then, when I declare
If you bump into one on the thoroughfare,
Or happen to stray into its lair,
Or trap it in a pit or a similar snare,
Or it eats your porridge or breaks your chair,
All I can say is you'd better beware.
Prepare yourself for a scary affair
That'll probably turn out a proper nightmare.
And it only takes one careless stare.

It only takes one careless stare
To make it mad and drive it spare
Cos a bear can't bear a human stare.
And worst of all is the grizzly bear
With claws that rip and slash and tear.
That's the grizzly truth, the grizzly truth,
The grizzly truth, I swear.

For your own welfare, best gaze elsewhere,
Like over here or over there,
Directly down at your leather footwear
Or up at the weather in the wind-blown air;
But never ever stare, no never ever stare,
Don't dare to stare at a grizzly bear
Cos a bear can't bear a human stare,
And worst of all is the grizzly bear.

It snorts and snarls. Its nostrils flare.
You haven't got a hope. You're beyond despair
Cos before you've time to say a prayer
It'll chew through you, chew through you,
Chew through you like a chocolate eclair.

Chew through you like a chocolate eclair,
Till you're just bare bones . . . and underwear.

Newt

It's better by far to own a newt
Than a bedbug or a bandicoot.
Truly, there's no substitute
For the ownership of a real live newt.

I'll tell you this. If I'd a newt
I'd feed it fish and free-range fruit,
French food freshly fried en croute,
Baked bean butties and boiled beetroot.

I'd dress my newt in a minute suit,
Shoving each claw in a wellington boot,
And every weekday he'd commute
To a management job at an institute.

In a war, my newt, as a raw recruit
Would learn to march and aim and shoot
And stand up straight and give a salute
And volunteer to execute
A daring raid by parachute.

And if life left me destitute,
My poverty utter and absolute . . .
Ah, well! I'd simply sell the brute
For a decent price cos he'd be a beaut.

And you getta lotta loot
You getta lotta loot
You getta lotta loot
For a newt that's cute.

Giving the Pope an Antelope

How do you cope?
How do you cope?
How do you cope
With an antelope?

It's not quite bright
But a big dumb dope
That'll impolitely
Grab and grope.

I can't cope.
I can't cope.
I can't cope
With my antelope.

It'll lazily graze
On a grassy slope
Or gaze for days
Down my telescope.

I raised my problem
With the Pope
Who praised its wobbling
Awkward lope.

He could cope.
He could cope.
He could cope
With an antelope.

I scrubbed mine down
In bubbly soap,
Tugged it around
On a length of a rope,

Took it to the Vatican.
When the Pope
Said: "Take it back again!"
I said: "Nope.
You're my last hope.

I know you'll cope.
I know you'll cope.
I know you'll cope
With my antelope."

The Pet Fanatic

Every morning, you awake
With cattle in your bed and a rattlesnake.
You take a dip in your swimming pool
With your hippopotamus and your mule.
Then you have breakfast on your lawn
In the company of a coastal prawn,
Before you fly off in your jet
To work in the city with your marmoset.

From your office, you e-mail
Daily poems to your favourite snail.
After that, you share a cab
With a vampire bat and a hermit crab.
Soon you're strolling through the park
Chatting with a vole and an old aardvark,
Or riding high in a horsedrawn coach
Sat by the side of a large cockroach.

For lunch you go to cocktail bars
Drinking punch with jaguars and a bunch of drunk tarantulas.
At your club, you then play bridge
With two chipmunks and a moody midge.
Next you go to a fashion show
With forty crows and a water buffalo.
At half-past-three, you take high tea
With a fly and a flea and a bumble bee.

Then perhaps to a picture-house
Watching a movie, sat with a mouse,
Having hot popcorn and a laugh
With a film-fan fawn and a pedigree giraffe;
(not to a play, cos plot and drama
bore your ocelot and your llama);
Then to a restaurant, sharing courses
With a polar bear and a pair of shire horses.

On the bus, you sit and discuss
Literature with an octopus.
Home at last and up the stairs.
You call goodnight to your grizzly bears
And to all your other teds
Who've said their prayers and are in their beds.
"Lights out!" shouts the armadillo.
Your head has hardly hit the pillow,
But the room has filled with counted sheep
And you're already fast asleep.

The Patient Lynx

The day's been hot. A patient lynx
Lies in the long grass. Waits. And thynx
Of waters lapping mud-bank brynx
Of pools, as heat-haze cools and shrynx.

And away to the west, a slow sun synx;
Its blood-red circle spilling pynx
Into the blue and purple ynx
Of evening sky where one star twynx.

Late shadows lengthen round the lynx.
At last, it lifts its head and blynx.
Then, cautiously, the creature slynx
To water's edge and, watchful, drynx.

Ted the Gorilla

Old Ted, the gorilla,
His head on his pillow,
Got iller and iller and iller.

Old Ted, the gorilla,
Though fed a germ-killer,
Got iller and iller and iller.

Old Ted, the gorilla,
His voice getting shriller,
Got iller and iller and iller.

Old Ted, the gorilla,
Though still a pill-swiller,
Got iller and iller and iller.

Old Ted, the gorilla,
Lay dead on his pillow
And never got iller
Or stiller or chiller,
No never got iller than that!

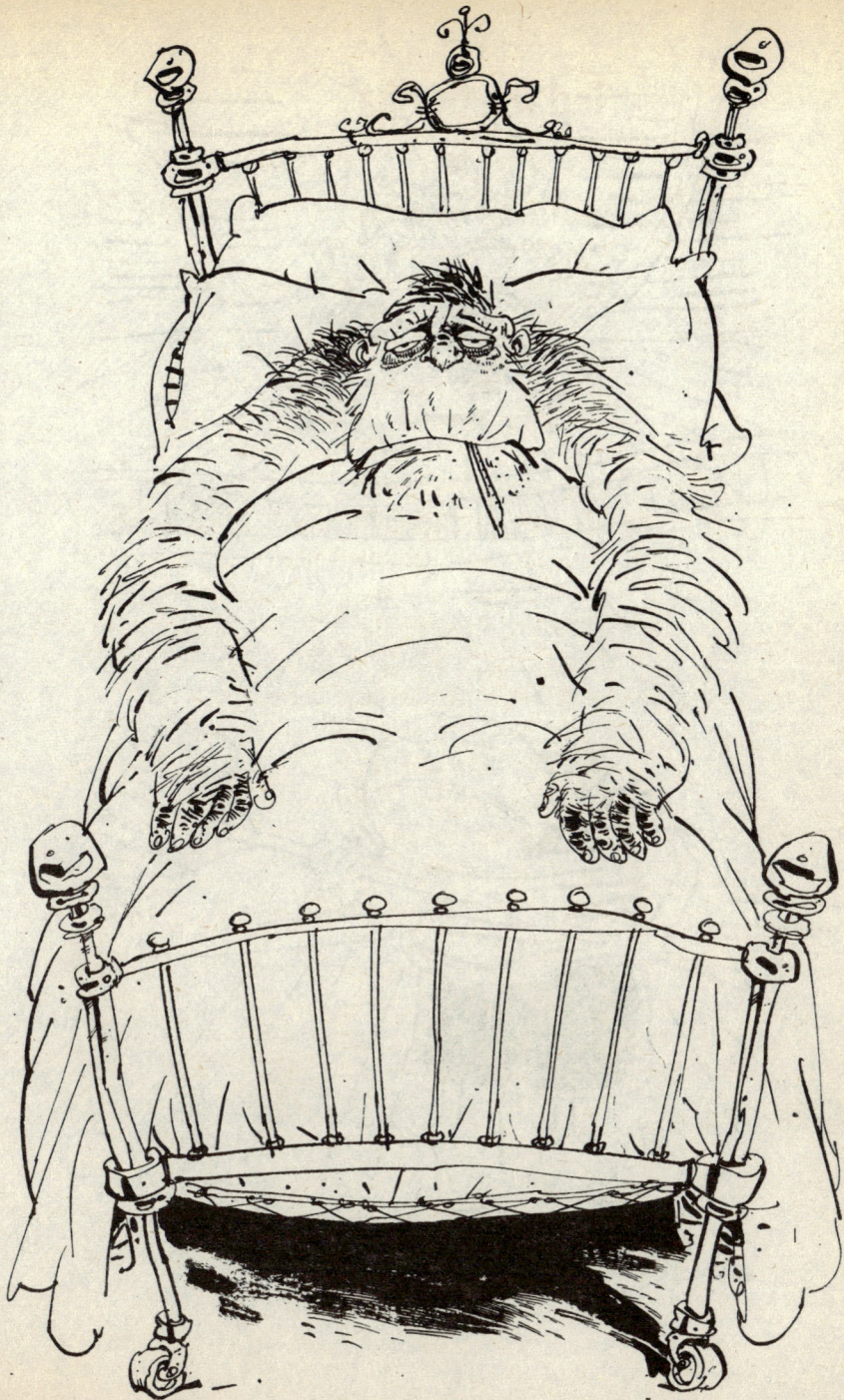

Rat in the Attic

Rat-a-tat-tat. Rat-a-tat-tat.
Rat up in the attic. Oh, listen to that.
Rattling around like an acrobat.
That pitter-pattering, clattering rat.

Rat-a-tat-tat. Rat-a-tat-tat.
We can't sleep. Here we're sat.
Never heard anything quite like that.
That pitter-pattering, clattering rat.

Rat-a-tat-tat. Rat-a-tat-tat.
Rat-a-tat-tat. Drat that rat!
Rat-a-tat-tat. Get the prat!
That pitter-pattering, clattering rat.

Rat-a-tat-tat. Rat-a-tat-tat.
Flatten that rat! Batter the brat!
Splatter that un-get-at-able rat!
That pitter-pattering, clattering rat.

Rat-a-tat-tat. Rat-a-tat-tat.
Rat up in the attic. Will you listen to that?
Rat-a-tat-tat. Rat-a-tat-tat.
Rat-a-tat-tat. Rat-a-tat-tat.
Rat-a-tat-tat. Rat-a-tat-tat.

Pig Ahoy!

I saw a pig,
A pig, pig, pig,
With a twirly tail
Like a whirligig,
Pack a picnic snack
In a thingamajig
And go for a sail
On a fisherhog's brig,
In a sailor-suit
And waterproof rig.

But the sea got rough.
The waves grew big,
With each one wearing
A white foam wig,
Till the boat was flung
In a final jig
And broke in bits
No bigger than a twig.
So the sea took a swig
And away went pig.

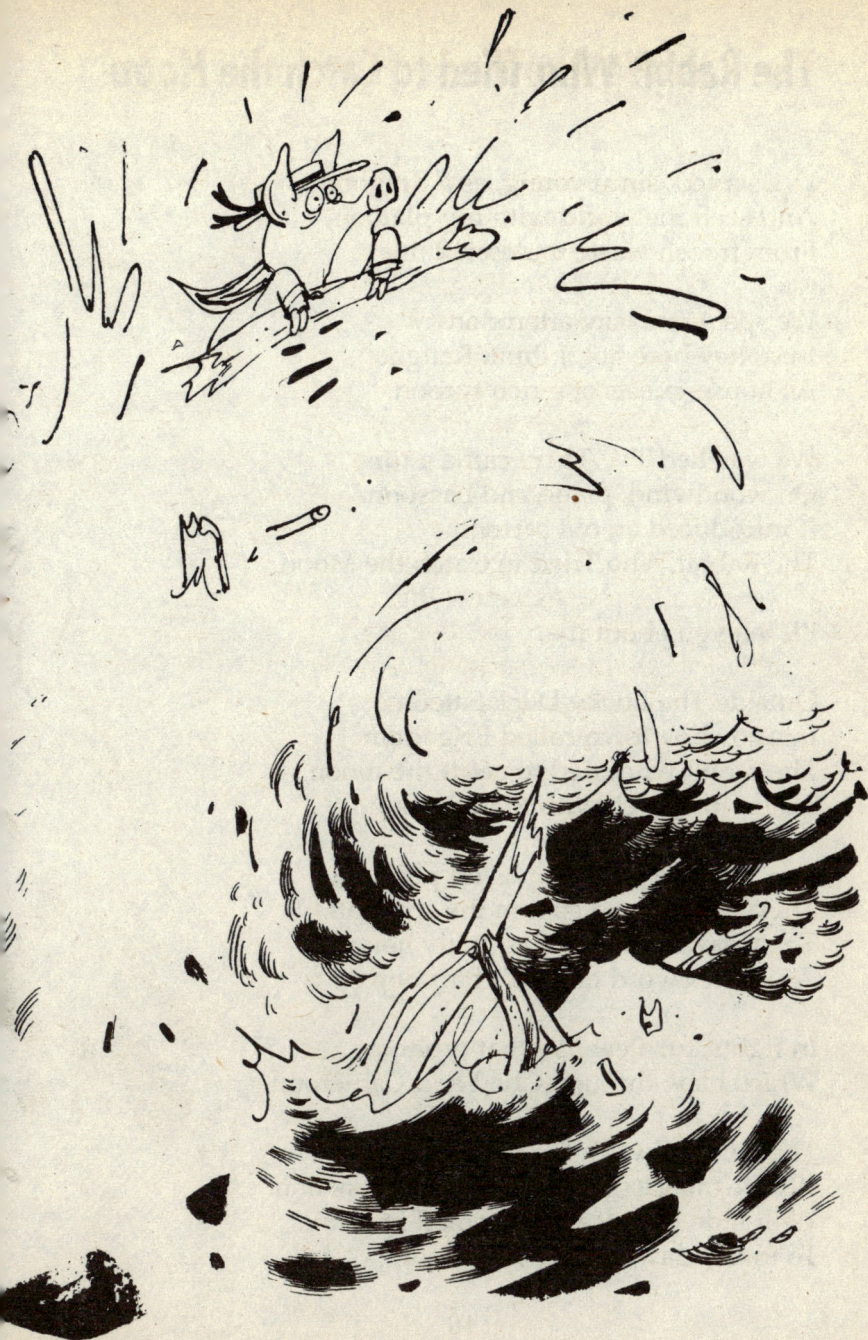

The Rabbit Who Tried to Catch the Moon

I've served, since young, as a dragoon
And seen the world with my platoon,
From frozen waste to desert dune.

We spent one lazy afternoon
In somewhere hot, I think Rangoon,
As house-guests of a rich tycoon.

We watched TV. There came a tune
On woodwind, piano and bassoon.
It introduced an old cartoon:
The Rabbit Who Tried to Catch the Moon.

I'll tell you about it . . .

Outside The Lucky Duck Saloon
In a cowboy town called Brigadoon
The rabbit who tried to catch the moon
Sat on the porch with Rick Racoon.

Inside, some tomcats played pontoon.
They howled and spat in the spittoon.
Their paws hid claws as finely hewn
As pirate sword or ship's harpoon.

In fights, fur flew like that typhoon
Which blew through Chad and Cameroon.

The barman was a big baboon
Whose muscles made the toughest swoon.
With hide like steel, he seemed immune
To tooth, claw, bullet or harpoon.

The rabbit who tried to catch the moon
Sat silently with Rick Racoon.
Above them shone the summer moon
As round and bright as a gold doubloon.

The air was warm, that night in June,
Like nest or den or silk cocoon;
The kind of night when street-cats croon,
The sort of sky that stars festoon,
A satin sheet, a deep lagoon
On which uncounted sparks are strewn.

The rabbit said to Rick Racoon:
"I'm going to catch myself that moon.
Its rare lamplight would be a boon.

I'll leap up there one night quite soon
When circumstance is opportune
And scoop it with a silver spoon."

This brought disdain from Rick Racoon:
"You nincompoop. You goofy goon.
You dunder-pated pantaloon.

A creature cannot own the moon.
It's not some kind of bright balloon;
Or grabbable, like a macaroon.

It's huge and far, you poor buffoon.
It's dark and dry, just like a prune,
And so's your brain, you loony-tune."

"But this ain't life, we're in a cartoon,"
the rabbit replied to Rick Racoon . . .

Then: "Let's get moving, B Platoon!"
"Yes, sir!" "Yes, sir, Sergeant Calhoon!"
And we missed the end of our cartoon,
Never knew whether he caught his moon.

The sun sank low and glowed maroon.
The season then was mid-monsoon.
We marched through mud, but hummed that tune
Of woodwind, piano and bassoon . . .
While over us rose a marvellous moon.

How the Bumble Bee Got His Stripes

On the day that the world began,
Each of the creatures was shown
All the colours of the universe;
And all were told to choose
Which of these they wanted for themselves.

Well, that day the elephant
Thought carefully and chose to be grey,
But the bumble bee
Just bumbled around and buzzed around
And couldn't make up his mind,
And the yellow sun shone so brightly
That the bumble bee's bum became yellow.

And that night the goldfish
Thought carefully and chose to be golden,
But the bumble bee
Just bumbled around and buzzed around
And couldn't make up his mind,
And the black night grew so dark
That the bumble bee's hips became black.

And next day the cricket
Thought carefully and chose to be green,
But the bumble bee
Just bumbled around and buzzed around
And couldn't make up his mind,
And the yellow sun shone so brightly
That the bumble bee's waist became yellow.

And that night the owl
Thought carefully and chose to be brown,
But the bumble bee
Just bumbled around and buzzed around
And couldn't make up his mind,
And the black night grew so dark
That the bumble bee's chest became black.

And next day the polar bear
Thought carefully and chose to be white,
But the bumble bee
Just bumbled around and buzzed around
And couldn't make up his mind,
And the yellow sun shone so brightly
That the bumble bee's shoulders became yellow.

And that night the jay
Thought carefully and chose to be blue,
But the bumble bee
Just bumbled around and buzzed around
And couldn't make up his mind,
And the black night grew so dark
That the bumble bee's neck and head and legs became black.

And next day the bumble bee
Began to be thoughtful.
He bumbled around and buzzed around
But thought carefully,
And chose the colours he wanted to be.
He said: "I've made up my mind.
I want to be all the colours of the rainbow."
But it was too late
Because the bumble bee
Had already become black striped
And yellow striped,
From the top of his head
To the tip of his toes.

Seasick

"I don't feel welk," whaled the squid, sole-fully.
"What's up?" asked the doctopus.
"I've got sore mussels and a tunny-hake," she told him.

"Lie down and I'll egg salmon you," mermaid the doctopus.
"Rays your voice," said the squid. "I'm a bit hard of herring."
"Sorry! I didn't do it on porpoise," replied the doctopus
    orc-wardly.

He helped her to oyster self onto his couch
And asked her to look up so he could sea urchin.
He soon flounder plaice that hurt.

"This'll make it eel," he said, whiting a prescription.
"So I won't need to see the sturgeon?" she asked.
"Oh, no," he told her. "In a couple of dace you'll feel brill."

"Cod bless you," she said.
"That'll be sick squid," replied the doctopus.

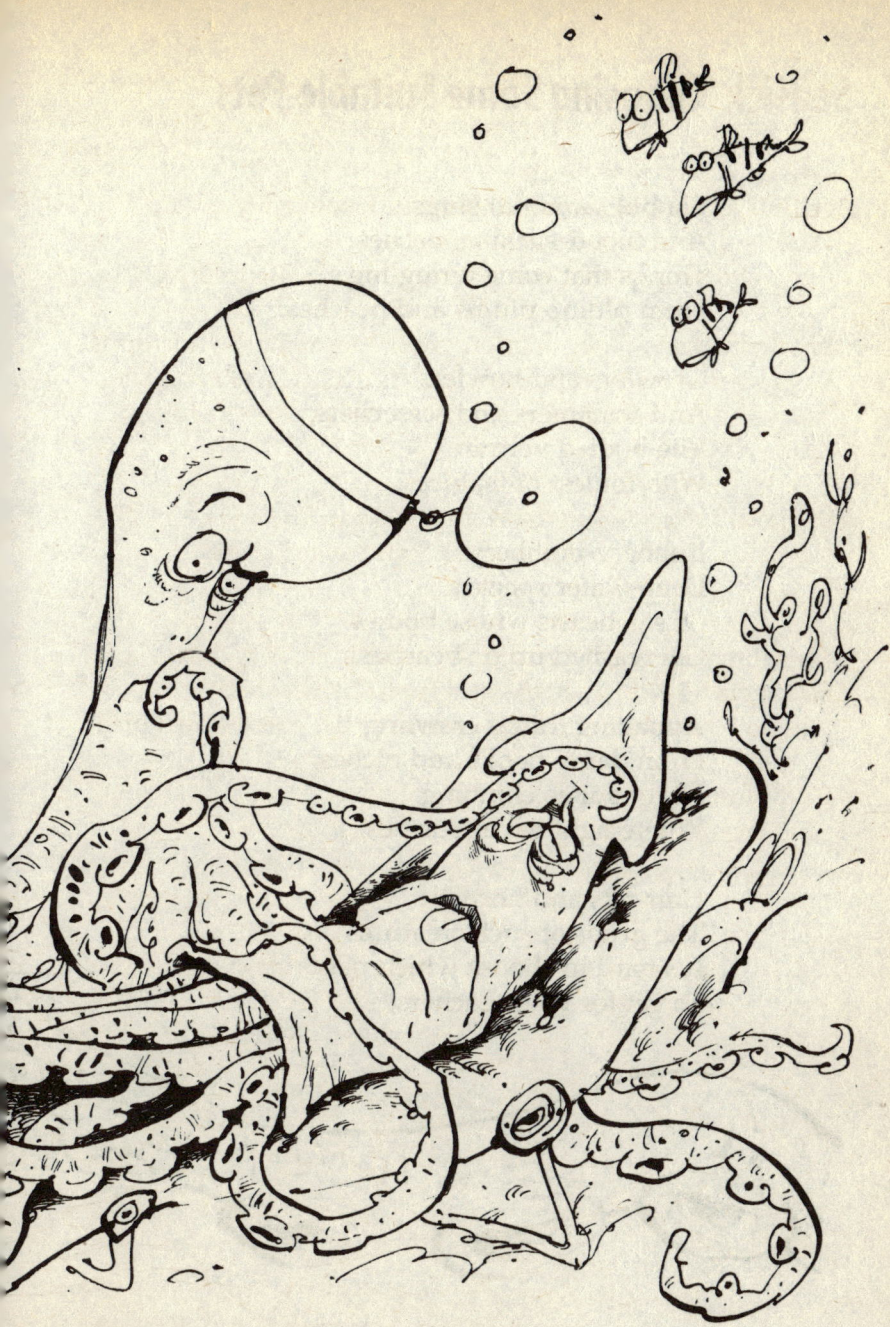

Choosing Some Suitable Pets

Big bugs and flat slugs
And blood-sucking leeches;
Things that come wriggling
From plump plums and peaches;

Growlers and howlers
And screamers and screechers;
Vile-bodied vermin
With foulest of features;

Rubbery, blubbery
Deep-water species
Of sea-beasts whose bodies
Get washed up on beaches;

Appalling things crawling
From damp nooks and niches;
Slimy things climbing
Where light never reaches;

Hair-nits and hornets;
The grubs of such creatures . . .
It's hard to choose which pets
To get for your teachers!

PTHRRRP!

Broose, My Moose

I caught a moose
And called him Broose.
I tied him with a few lassoose
Securely to a towering sproose.

I groomed my moose
With grease of goose
And soaps and scents the French prodoose
And oily inks of octopoose.

I loved that moose
What was the yoose?
He ate my meals. He drank my joose,
But gave back only moose aboose

Can you dedoose
Quite why my moose
Was so ungrateful and obtoose?
Perhaps he was a few scroose loose.

I'd introdoose
You all to Broose
But can't do so, cos he broke loose
By chewing through each ropy noose.

Don't ask why Broose
Chose to vamoose.
He gave no reason or excoose.
Perhaps I'd caught the wrong moose.
Next time, I'll get a mongoose.

Life, there's nothing stranger than it.
So it was an interplanet-
ary spaceship with, to man it,
men with heads like pomegranate-

s, came to visit Mr Hannett.
Now the council simply cannot
part the teacher from his gannet.
Both live on another planet.

Alphabet Zoo

1.

ABC: the water buffalee
DEF: the chimpanzeff
GHI: the anacondeye
JKL: the bird of paradell
MNO: the hippopotamo
PQR: the porcupar
STU: the butterflew
VW: the chameleoo
XYZ: the kangared

2.

ABC: the African elephanee
DEF: the wildebeff
GHI: the polar bye
JKL: the octopell
MNO: the spiny ant-eatoe
PQR: the rhinocerar
STU: the crocadoo
VW: the budgerigoo
XYZ: the tarantuled.

(N.B. If you're American, and say 'zee' instead of 'zed', it'd
be 'kangaree' and 'tarantulee'.)

Talkative Cows

Have you heard the tittle-tattle
From a chatty herd of cattle?

Chewing cud and chewing fat'll
Set the tongues of cows a-rattle.

Each'll natter, each'll prattle,
Chatter like a diplomat'll.

When they row, there's little that'll
End their bitter verbal battle.

So, if you can hush these cattle,
I'll not only eat my hat, I'll
Swim from Scarborough to Seattle!

Where Does That Dingo Go?

No one knows where the dingo goes
Ahead of its tail, but behind its nose.

It must go somewhere, I suppose,
Though I know nobody who knows.
And so this problem first arose
As a mystery that no one chose.

No one knows where the dingo goes
Ahead of its tail, but behind its nose.

It breezes in but won't disclose
Where it's been before it shows.
It stays a while, then away it blows
With no goodbyes or cheerios.

No one knows where the dingo goes
Ahead of its tail, but behind its nose.

This dog doggedly tos and fros,
Says no yeses, says no noes
To all the questions which we pose.
Curiosity overflows!

No one knows where the dingo goes
Ahead of its tail, but behind its nose.

Sleuths line up in rows and rows.
They're knocked down like dominoes.
No detectives can expose
Where dingo sneaks on tippy-toes.

No one knows where the dingo goes
Ahead of its tail, but behind its nose.

A case no Sherlock Holmes can close,
Nor can Maigrets or Clouseaus,
Or Father Browns, Hercule Poirots,
Or Scotland Yard, or all of those
Employed by Federal Bureaux.

No one knows where the dingo goes
Ahead of its tail, but behind its nose.

It's a riddle that grows and grows and grows.

The Price of Worms

Well, what on earth
Is an earthworm worth?
Would you swap one worm
For a modicum of mirth?
For a third of a word
Or a fourth of firth?

For a part of a port
To the north of Perth?
Or a three-berth boat?
Or a nine-pence note?
Or a fish-fur coat
Of enormous girth?

What if worms were rare?
What if there was a dearth
When a whole lot of earthworms
Died at birth?
Then perhaps one worm
Would cost the earth.

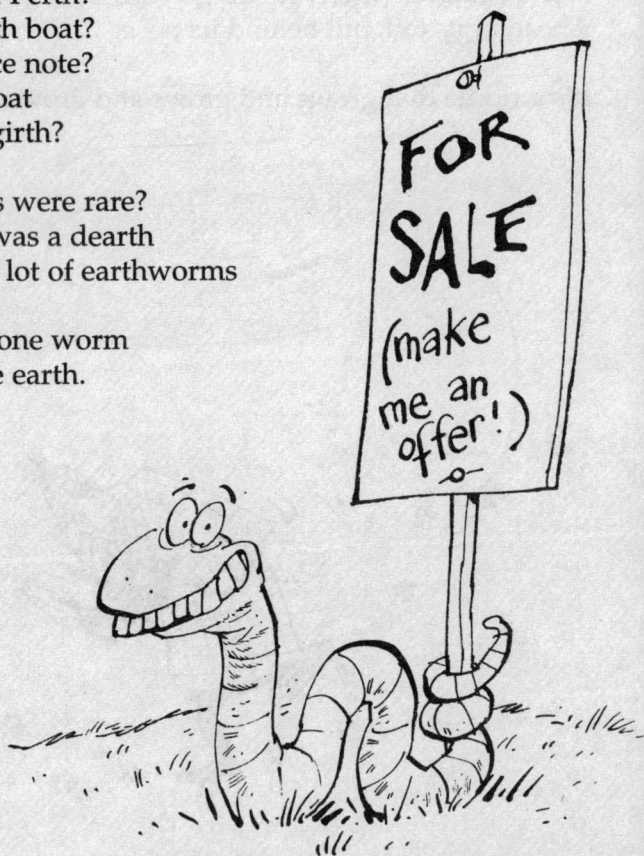

FOR
SALE
(make
me an
offer!)

Getting a Goldfish

We bought ourselves a goldfish
From a Polish man who sold fish.
It's a very cold-to-hold fish,
On slow patrol
Around its bowl.
I'm told it's quite an old fish.

Sniff!

Treating Chimps

Chimpanzeeses catch diseases
Such as sniffles, such as sneezes,
Such as coffles, such as wheezes.
Wrap 'em well when winter freezes.

Chimpanzeeses catch diseases
When they're left in drafts and breezes . . .
They get pain that grips and seizes.
Ease it all with hugs and squeezes.

Chimpanzeeses catch diseases
Queasiness that nags and teases.
All the usual food displeases.
Feed them chick-peas, chives and cheeses.

Chimpanzeeses catch diseases
Get uneases in their kneeses
From the bites of mites and fleases.
Pick these bugs out using tweezers.
Rub unsightly sores with greases.

These is ways we treats diseases
Which get caught by chimpanzeeses.

The Turkey

Just how this odd bird has occurred
Has only been vaguely inferred.
Its history's a mystery
That's murky and blurred.
The turkey's a circus-freak sort of a bird:
A creature created cos nature has erred.

This geek with a beak that's unique
Is a bird that's completely absurd.
There's no other word
The turkey's a nerd.
It's totally quirky.
Its movements are jerky.
Its cry is the strangest I've heard.

It waddles along looking perky,
But its shape is berserk.
It's the bird's bodywork
That is more than just slightly
Ungainly, unsightly,
This turkey's a nerd of a bird.

Ask the feathered, the finned and the furred
In flock or in shoal or in herd.
They all know that nerd's
The appropriate word,
The word that's quite rightly
– although impolitely –
Conferred on a bird so absurd
And gawky and jerky and awkwardly quirky . . .

Yes, we're talking turkey:
That berk of a bird
Gone gobbledy-squawky
And portly-to-porky
And can't-properly-walky
And wings-what-won't-worky.

The turkey's just half of a third of a bird
Constructed by one who'd not heard of a bird
Cos a turkey's a berk of a nerd of a bird.

Peter the Cheetah

Here's Peter the champion cheetah
Well fed on the meat of
A freshly-killed bleater.
It's Peter the champion cheetah.

No running-style sweeter,
No pacing that's neater.
It's Peter the champion cheetah.

The fastest competer
At 800 metres
It's Peter the champion cheetah.

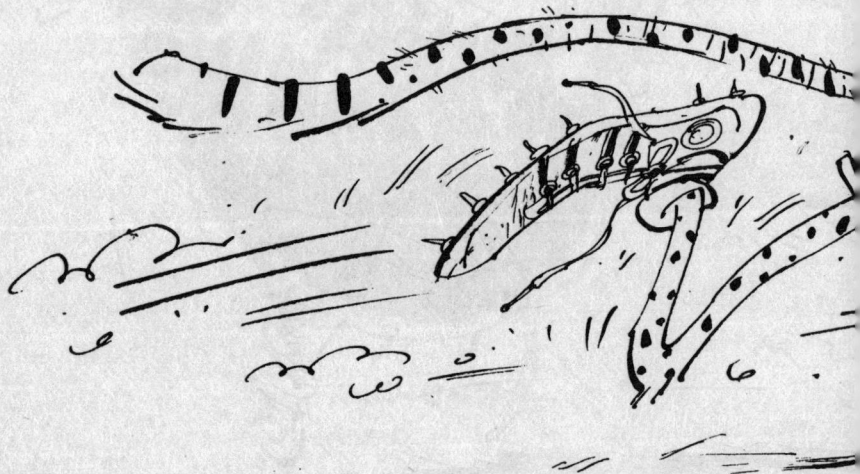

A race-goer's treat and
A loping lap-eater.
It's Peter the champion cheetah.

A feline world-beater,
Few creatures are fleeter
Than Peter the champion . . .
Peter the champion . . .
Peter the champion cheetah.

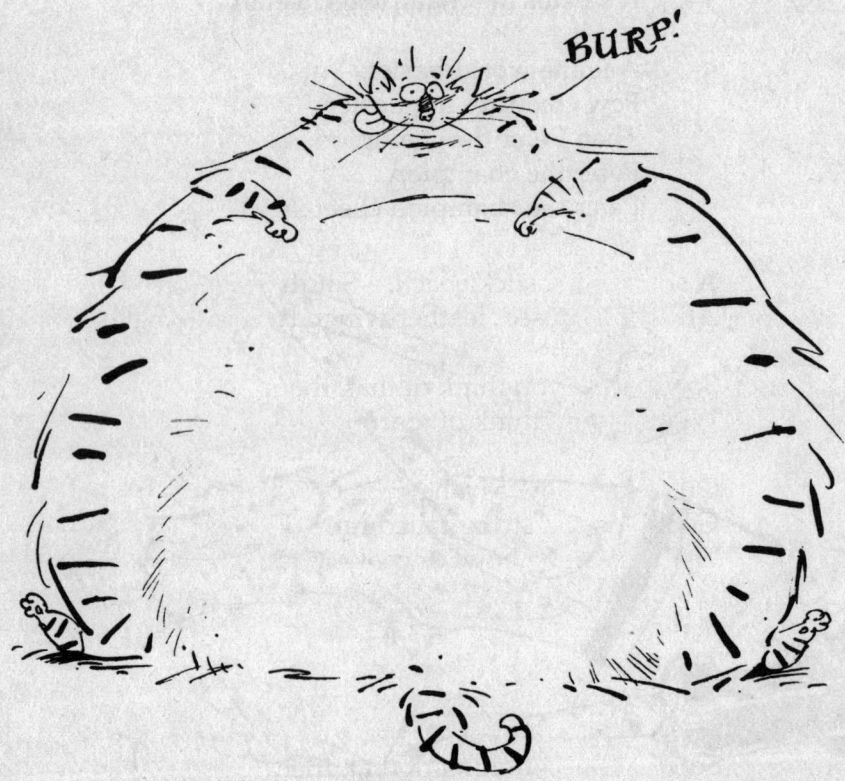

Greedy Cat

Our cat, hollow as a hat,
Gobbled up a string-tailed rat
And the whole of a bowl of cooking fat.

So what do you think of that, then?
What do you think of that?

Our cat, hollow as a hat,
Gobbled up a string-tailed rat,
The whole of a bowl of cooking fat,
A sturgeon, a stickleback, a South Sea sprat
And a pig-nosed, leather-winged vampire bat.

So what do you think of that, then?
What do you think of that?

Our cat, hollow as a hat,
Gobbled up a string-tailed rat,
The whole of a bowl of cooking fat,
A sturgeon, a stickleback, a South Sea sprat,
A pig-nosed, leather-winged vampire bat,
A starling, a redstart, a dead stonechat,
A big bluebottle and a tiny gnat.

So what do you think of that, then?
What do you think of that?

Our cat, hollow as a hat,
Gobbled up a string-tailed rat,
The whole of a bowl of cooking fat,
A sturgeon, a stickleback, a South Sea sprat,
A pig-nosed, leather-winged vampire bat,
A starling, a redstart, a dead stonechat,
A big bluebottle, a tiny gnat,
A mango, a paw-paw, a ripe kumquat
And a road-kill rabbit that was very, very, very, very, very,
very flat.

So what do you think of that, then?
What do you think of that?

The Day Our Teacher Took Her Pet to School

Oh, that was a day that we'll never forget,
And one our poor teacher will always regret.
What set our whole class in a terrible sweat
Was the creature that teacher described as her pet.

At lunchtime that day in the infants' toilet,
They found what was left of a smoked cigarette.
The head blamed a pupil, but it's a safe bet
That the one who had done it was our teacher's pet.

It challenged us all to a game of roulette;
Won our dinner money. We've not eaten yet.
And each of the teachers is deeply in debt
To the champion gambler that's our teacher's pet.

The caretaker chased it around with a net
Till it was as angry as animals get.
Then, down in the playground, the two of them met
And the human got eaten by our teacher's pet.

They say music's soothing when beasts are upset,
But this one found most tunes a bit of a threat.
There wasn't much left of the school string-quartet
When they played Beethoven to our teacher's pet.

It chewed through three pupils who played clarinet
But, while it was dining on a drum-majorette,
We lowered a noose from a high parapet,
Thereby roping and capturing our teacher's pet.

We took it to be put down by our local vet;
But it ate him, a parrot, a pet marmoset,
A beagle, a budgie, an ailing egret,
And a litter of kittens, did our teacher's pet.

The details appeared in *The Evening Gazette*.
Later that night though, an airforce cadet
At the RAF base saw a dark silhouette
Of a shape very similar to our teacher's pet.

At midnight our school was bombed flat by a jet,
Reduced to mere rubble by one Exocet.
The head blamed a terrorist gang from Tibet,
But all of us knew it was our teacher's pet.

Noggin-the-Nog

Meet our dog: Noggin-the-Nog,
Probably the world's most ancient dog.

He's blind as a bat, with eyes like fog;
Lies in the lane like a fallen log
With a brain Dad says has lost a cog
And a bark that's like a strangled frog.

Noggin-the-Nog, Noggin-the-Nog,
Probably the world's most ancient dog.

He's chewed up the Argos catalogue,
Mum's slipper, my shoe, and Grandad's clog.
He waits for the postman, all agog,
Then sees him off at a jaunty jog.

Noggin-the-Nog, Noggin-the-Nog,
Probably the world's most ancient dog.

Living with him is a thankless slog.
He's more grumpy than an old hedgehog
And smells like The Beast from Bodmin Bog;
Not the sort of dog that pet shops flog.

Noggin-the-Nog, Noggin-the-Nog,
Probably the world's most ancient dog.

The Dragon Who Ate Our School

Poems by Nick Toczek

The day the dragon came to call
she ate the gate, the playground wall
and, slate by slate, the roof and all,
the staffroom, gym and entrance hall.

And every classroom, big or small.

So...
She's undeniably great.
She's absolutely cool,
the dragon who ate
the dragon who ate
the dragon who ate our school.

Dragons Everywhere

Poems by Nick Toczek

The Dragon in the Cellar

There's a dragon!
There's a dragon!
There's a dragon in the cellar!
Yeah, we've got a cellar-dweller.
There's a dragon in the cellar.

He's a cleanliness fanatic,
takes his trousers and his jacket
to the dragon in the attic
who puts powder by the packet
in a pre-set automatic
with a rattle and a racket
that's disturbing and dramatic.

There's a dragon!
There's a dragon!
There's a dragon in the cellar
with a flame that's red 'n' yeller.
There's a dragon in the cellar . . .

A selected list of poetry books available from Macmillan

The prices shown below are correct at the time of going to press. However, Macmillan Publishers reserve the right to show new retail prices on covers which may differ from those previously advertised.

The Dragon Who Ate Our School 0 330 34829 9
Fire-breathing poems, by Nick Toczek £3.50

Dragons Everywhere 0 330 36792 7
More fire-breathing poems, by Nick Toczek £3.50

Dracula's Auntie Ruthless 0 330 33388 7
And other petrifying poems, chosen by David Orme £2.99

Nothing Tastes Quite Like a Gerbil 0 330 34632 6
And other vile verses, chosen by David Orme £2.99

The Secret Lives of Teachers 0 330 34265 7
Revealing rhymes, chosen by Brian Moses £3.50

'Ere We Go! 0 330 32986 3
Football poems, chosen by David Orme £2.99

You'll Never Walk Alone 0 330 33787 4
More football poems, chosen by David Orme £2.99

All Macmillan titles can be ordered at your local bookshop or are available by post from:

Book Service by Post
PO Box 29, Douglas, Isle of Man IM99 1BQ

Credit cards accepted. For details:
Telephone: 01624 675137
Fax: 01624 670923
E-mail: bookshop@enterprise.net

Free postage and packing in the UK.
Overseas customers: add £1 per book (paperback)
and £3 per book (hardback).